CONGRATULATIONS!

So Proud!

ADVENTURE MONEY

Well Done!

MUNCHIE MONEY

Success!

PLAY MONEY

Celebrate!

Gas Money

You Did It!

FUN MONEY

Woohoo!

Celebration Money

Kudos!

PIZZA MONEY

Great Accomplishment

Party Money

Smart!

Sharing Money

Well Deserved!

Enjoyment Money

ENJOY!

Go Celebrate!

Library of Congress Control Number: Fun Times
Paper Back ISBN 978-1-944923-12-9
Hardcover ISBN 978-1-944923-13-6

Because of the dynamic nature of the content herein, any money contained in this book may have changed since publication.
Enjoy & Congratulations!

154 Easy Street
Carol Stream, IL 60188

Other Best Money Books:

- For a Great Guy
- For a Great Girl
- For a Princess
- For the New Mother
- For the Superhero
- For the Newlyweds
- For a New Home
- For You – Special Occasion
- New Baby
- For a Special Person

www.ingramcontent.com/pod-product-compliance
Lightning Source LLC
Chambersburg PA
CBHW081137300726
48982CB00005B/981

* 9 7 8 1 9 4 4 9 2 3 1 3 6 *